Anonymous

The History, Standing Rúles

Anatiposi

Anonymous

The History, Standing Rúles

Reprint of the original, first published in 1871.

1st Edition 2023 | ISBN: 978-3-38212-474-8

Anatiposi Verlag is an imprint of Outlook Verlagsgesellschaft mbH.

Verlag (Publisher): Outlook Verlag GmbH, Zeilweg 44, 60439 Frankfurt, Deutschland
Vertretungsberechtigt (Authorized to represent): E. Roepke, Zeilweg 44, 60439 Frankfurt, Deutschland
Druck (Print): Books on Demand GmbH, In de Tarpen 42, 22848 Norderstedt, Deutschland

THE

HISTORY, STANDING RULES,

Confession of Faith,

COVENANT & MEMBERS

OF THE

Maple Street Congregational Church,

IN

DANVERS, MASS.,

——:o:——

COMPILED BY ORDER OF THE CHURCH, AND EXTENDING
TO MAY, 1871.

——:o:——

SALEM:
OBSERVER STEAM JOB PRINTING ROOMS.
1871.

HISTORICAL.

THE Third Congregational Church in Danvers, was constituted December 5th, 1844, at the house of Brother John A. Learoyd, and consisted of forty-two members, thirteen males, and twenty-nine females, most of whom were by their request dismissed from the First Church in Danvers. The public exercises were held in Granite Hall, and Rev. Brown Emerson, D. D., of Salem, preached the sermon on the occasion. At a meeting of the Brethren, held December 4th, 1844, Brothers Frederic Howe and Samuel P. Fowler were chosen Deacons, and on July 15th, 1864, Brother John S. Learoyd was added to the number. April 30th, 1857, the name of the Church was changed to the Maple Street Church, in conformity to a vote of the Society.

The first Pastor, Rev. Richard Tolman, was ordained September 17th, 1845, and resigned his office November 8th, 1848. The second Pastor, Rev. James Fletcher, was ordained June 20th, 1849, and resigned his pastoral office May 21st, 1864. The third Pastor, Rev. William Carruthers, was installed April 18th, 1866, and resigned his pastorate March 28th, 1868. The fourth and pres-

ent Pastor, Rev. James Brand, was ordained Octobe
6th, 1869. The twenty-fifth anniversary of the forma
tion of the Church was held on the evening of the 5tl
of December, 1869, when a history of the Church anc
Society was given by one of its members. At that time
the membership of the Church was 207, and from thai
date to May 7th, 1871, there were added 70, making
the whole number at present 277.

RULES.

———

I.   The officers of the Church shall be the Pastor and Deacons.   The Deacons shall be chosen by ballot when vacancies occur.

II.   An annual meeting of the Church shall be held on the first Friday in April; at which time, a statement shall be made in writing, by the Pastor or Deacons, of the number of persons received into the Church during the year, by letter and by profession; of the number dismissed, deceased, or disciplined; of the number baptized; of the whole number of the Church; male and female; of the names of the members of the Church who may have removed from the place; of the condition of the Sabbath School; of the state of religion during the year, and other objects of general religious interest, all of which statements shall be entered upon the records of the Church.

III.   The expenses of the Church are to be defrayed by a contribution at each communion season, and, of all money so received, the Deacons are to have charge and to make report thereof at the annual meeting.

IV.   The Pastor, with the Deacons and such other members of the Church as may be chosen, shall be a committee to examine candidates for admission to the Church; also to receive, manage and present to the Church all cases of discipline.

V. Candidates for admission to the Church shall have given to them, a copy of the Articles and Covenant; be examined upon the same, and approved by the committee or the Church; be propounded two weeks before the communion; and assent in public to the Articles and Covenant.

Persons received by letter from other churches, shall, at some meeting of the Church, signify their assent to the Articles and Covenant, and be admitted by a vote of the Church.

VI. Members of this Church removing to other places, are expected to take certificates of membership; and if they remain more than a year, to take letters of dismission to some other church, unless satisfactory reasons be given why they should not. And members of other churches worshiping with us more than a year, will be expected to remove their church relation to us, unless there be special reasons for delay.

VII. All meetings of the Church for business shall be opened with prayer.

VIII. Each member is expected to attend all the stated lectures and meetings of the Church.

IX. The Sacrament of the Lord's Supper shall be administered on the first Sabbath in January, March,

May, July, September and November. The preparatory lecture will be delivered on the Friday evening preceding.

X. The Monthly Concert of Prayer for Missions shall be observed on the first Sabbath evening, and the Sabbath School Concert on the second Sabbath evening of each month.

XI. The Pastor, when present, shall preside at all meetings of the Church.

XII. The Clerk shall record all doings of the Church, and keep on file all the papers belonging to the Church.

XIII. The Sisters of the Church are expected to attend all its meetings, whether for business or devotion.

XIV. No alteration shall be made in the Rules, the Confession of Faith, nor the Covenant, except by vote of two-thirds of the members present at a meeting regularly called—such alteration having been submitted in writing at a previous meeting.

A rule, however, may be temporarily suspended by a majority vote of the members present at any regular meeting.

FORM OF RECEPTION.

DEAR FRIENDS:

You present yourselves in this public manner to confess Christ before men, and to enter into covenant with God and with this Church. As the ground of our hope and love, we acknowledge the following Articles of Faith.

CONFESSION OF FAITH.

I. We believe in one only living and true God, infinite in every perfection, who subsists in three Persons: the Father, Son, and Holy Ghost; the Sovereign Disposer of all creatures and events, and the only proper object of religious worship.

II. We believe the Scriptures of the Old and New Testaments are given by the inspiration of the Holy Ghost, as the perfect and only rule of religious faith and practice.

III. We believe that God made man upright and holy, but that by disobedience he fell from that estate, and that in consequence of the fall, he involved himself and all his posterity in a state of sin and spiritual death.

IV. We believe that mankind are not left to perish in this state, but, through the sufferings and death of the Son of God, pardon and salvation are promised to all who repent and believe in Christ.

V. We believe that man, being by nature destitute of holiness, would never of himself be willing to accept the gracious offers of salvation, and therefore except a man be called, and renewed by the Holy Spirit, he can not be saved.

VI. We believe that the Holy Ghost, in perfect consistency with man's freedom, regenerates the souls of those whom God has given to his Son, sanctifies them through the truth, and keeps them through faith unto salvation.

VII. We believe that God has established a Church in the world, with which it is the duty of all true believers to become united; that the sacraments of the Church are Baptism and the Lord's Supper; that the believers in regular Church fellowship are the only proper communicants at the Lord's Supper, and that visible believers and their children are the only proper subjects of Baptism.

VIII. We believe that at the end of the world there will be a resurrection of the dead and a final judgment, when the wicked will go away into everlasting punishment, and the righteous into life eternal.

Do you thus believe?

[Candidates for Baptism assenting to this Creed, will then be baptized.]

THE COVENANT.

You, and each of you, depending upon the grace of God to enable you to keep this Covenant, do freely choose the Lord Jehovah to be your God ; the Son, as Prophet, Priest and King, to be your Saviour ; and the Holy Spirit to be your Sanctifier and Comforter.

You now covenant with God to give yourselves to him, with all you have and are, promising by the help of divine grace, to renounce the vanities of the world ; to resist sin and temptation, and obey all the commandments and ordinances of God ; to attend to the seals of the Covenant, Baptism and the Lord's Supper ; to attend and maintain the worship of God in his house, in your family (so far as depends on you), and in your closet ; to walk with this Church in christian fellowship ; to watch over its members, and submit to its discipline, as enjoined in the Gospel ; to seek the peace, purity and enlargement of this and all our sister Churches ; and finally, depending on God alone for strength, you promise to forget the things that are behind, and press on toward perfection, and never cease watching, praying and striving, till you come to the holiness of Heaven.

To this Covenant do you seriously consent ?

We, then, the members of this Church, (*here the*

members of the Church rise,) do affectionately receive you to our communion and fellowship, and, on our part, engage to watch over your spiritual interests, and walk with you in all the ordinances of the Gospel, with the spirit of meekness, love and tenderness, as becometh saints.

Now, beloved, you have vowed unto the Lord and cannot go back. These vows will be upon you wherever you go. They will follow you to the bar of God, and in whatever world you are fixed, will be upon you to eternity.

May the Lord guide and preserve you till death ; may the Lord make his face to shine upon you ; and at last receive you and us, through the merits of Christ, to the everlasting fellowship of the saints and angels. in the presence of the Father, the Son, and the Holy Ghost. *Amen.*

PASTORS AND OFFICERS OF THE CHURCH.

Rev. RICHARD TOLMAN.

Ordained Sept. 17, 1845. . . . . . *Resigned Nov. 8, 1848*

Rev. JAMES FLETCHER.

Ordained June 20, 1849. . . . . . *Resigned May 21, 186*

Rev. WILLIAM CARRUTHERS.

Installed April 18, 1866. . . . . . *Resigned March 28, 1868.*

Rev. JAMES BRAND.

Ordained Oct. 6, 1869.

—:o:—

DEACONS.

Frederick Howe, ...	Elected Dec. 4, 1844.
Samuel P. Fowler, ...	Elected Dec. 4, 1844.
John S. Learoyd, ...	Elected July 15, 1864.

CHRONOLOGICAL RECORD.

CHRONOLOGICAL RECORD OF MEMBERS.

[Where the State is not designated, it is understood, in *all* cases, that the town referred to is in Massachusetts. *Abbreviations*:—Let. Letter; fr. from; Cong. Congregational; M. E. Methodist Episcopal; dis. dismissed.

Reg.	Names.	Date of Recep'n.	How Received.		Date of Removal.	How Removed.
		1844.				
1	Samuel P. Fowler............	Dec. 5,	Letter from First Church.			
2	Frederic Howe..............	5,	do.	do.		
3	Warren Sheldon.............	5,	do.	do.		
4	Joseph S. Black.............	5,	do.	do.	Jan. 3, '61,	Death.
5	Moses W. Putnam...........	5,	do.	do.	Nov. 29, '55,	Dis. to ch. in Haverhill,
6	Francis P. Putnam..........	5,	do.	do.		
7	Jonathan Perry.............	5,	do.	do.	Nov. 16, '45,	Death.
8	Hezekiah Woodbury........	5,	do.	do.	July 6, '51,	Dis. to First Church.
9	Samuel Harris, Jr...........	5,	do.	do.		
10	John A. Learoyd	5,	do.	do.		
11	Moses J. Currier............	5,	do.	do.		
12	Benj. Turner...............	5,	do.	do.		
13	Nathaniel Silvester...... ...	5,	do.	do.	May 4, '55,	Dis. to ch. in Malden.

	Mrs. Harriet F.	Dec.	5,			
15	Mrs. Fidelia Endicott........		5,	do.	do.	Sept. 11, '54,	Death.
16	Mrs. Nancy E. Osgood.......		5,	do.	do.	Sept. 6, '69,	Death.
17	Mrs. Mary W. Howe.........		5,	do.	do.		
18	Mrs. Fanny Brown.........		5,	do.	do.		
19	Mrs. Mary H. Sheldon.......		5,	do.	do.	Sept. 13, '66,	Death.
20	Mrs. Betsy Putnam.........		5,	do.	do.	Oct. 23, '64,	Death.
21	Mrs. Susan H. Putnam......		5,	do.	do.		
22	Mrs. Emeline P. Black......		5,	do.	do.		
23	Mrs. Mary Putnam.........		5,	do.	do.	Feb. 23, '69,	Death.
24	Almira A. Putnam.........		5,	do.	do	July 2, '54,	Dis. to ch. in George-town.
25	Elizabeth H. Putnam.......		5,	do.	do.	Dec. 30, '64,	Death.
26	Mrs. Mary P. Trask........		5,	do.	do.		
27	Mrs. Nancy Kent...........		5,	do.	do.	March 5, '54,	Dis. to ch in Wenham.
28	Mrs. Emeline P. Fowle......		5,	do.	do.	April 27, '52,	Death.
29	Mrs. Susan Fuller.........		5,	do.	do.		
30	Mrs. Pamelia F. Putnam....		5,	do.	do.		
31	Mrs. Rebekah W. Perry.....		5,	do.	do.	May 13, 57,	Death.

Chronological Record of Members—Continued.

Reg.	Names.	Date of Recep'n.	How Received.	Date of Removal.	How Removed.
32	Harriet Perry..............	Dec. 5,	do. do.	Sept. 5, '56,	Dis. to ch. in Bedford.
33	Mrs. Eliza Woodbury........	5,	do. do.	July 6, '51,	Dis. to First Church.
34	Mrs. Lydia Harris..........	5,	do. do.		
35	Mrs. Eunice Putnam........	5,	do. do.		
36	Mrs. Sarah Learoyd........	5,	do. do.		
37	Mrs. Nancy P. Fisher........	5,	do. do.	Oct. 9, '63,	Dis. to First Church.
38	Mrs. Elizabeth C. Bateman..	5,	do. do.	Oct. 20, '49,	Death.
39	Mrs. Ruth P. Currier........	5,	do. do.		
40	Mrs. Charlotte H. Turner....	5,	do. do.		
41	Mrs. Lydia Silvester........	5,	do. do.	July, 28, '54,	Death.
42	Mrs. Harriet H. Elliot.......	5,	do. do.		
43	Mrs. Eunice P. Putnam.....	**1845.** Feb. 28,	Let. from ch. in Reading.		
44	Moody Elliot..............	Mar. 10,	Profession. . . .	May 31, '67,	Death.
45	Jesse Putnam.........	May 11,	Letter from First Church.	Feb. 9, '61,	Death.

No.	Name	Admitted	Mode	Removed	Manner
46	Allen Knight	May 11,	Letter from First Church,		
47	Mrs. Elizabeth Putnam	11,	do do		
48	Martha A. Putnam	11,	do do	July 22, '49,	Dis to ch. in Chelsea.
49	Mrs. Catharine P. Ober	11,	do do	Dec. 31, '52,	Dis. to ch. in Beverly.
50	Nathan Tapley	26,	do do	May 30, '71,	Death.
51	Mrs. Eliza Tapley	26,	Letter.	Sept. 18, '62,	Death.
52	Mrs. Elizabeth B. Granville.	Oct. 4,	Let. fr. Tab. ch., Salem.		
53	Julia Weston	Dec. 5, 1846.	Profession	Oct. 31, '48,	Dis. to ch. in Lynn.
54	Mrs. Olivia S. Tolman	Jan. 4,	Let. from ch. in Reading.	April 22, '49,	Dis. to ch. in So. Dennis, Mass.
55	Mrs. Betsey Marden	4,	Let. fr. Moultenboro', N.H.		
56	Mrs. Sophia Clement	4,	do do		
57	Mrs. Jane Bomer	4,	do do		
58	Frederic Perley	Feb. 8,	Let. fr. ch. in Topsfield.		
59	Mrs. Almira Perley	8,	do do		
60	Almira Perley	8,	do do	Oct. 10, '52,	Dis. to Crombie St. ch. in Salem.
61	James M. Perry	1847. Jan. 1,	Letter from First Church.		
62	Mrs. Caroline H. Perry	1,	do do		
	Samuel Wilson	1848. Feb. 20,	Let. fr. South ch., Danvers.		

Chronological Record of Members—Continued.

Reg.	Names.	Date of Recep'n.	How Received.		Date of Removal.	How Removed.
		1848.				
64	Mrs. Mary Wilson..........	Feb. 20,	Let. fr. South ch., Danvers,			
65	Ellen L. Putnam...........	Nov. 3,	Profession			
66	Helen E. Wilkins..........	3,	do.	do.	May 11, '62,	Excluded.
67	Elizabeth J. Bomer........	3,	do.	do.		
68	Abby M. Clement..........	3,	do.	do.		
69	Mary Fish................	3,	do.	do.		
70	Harriet A. Putnam........	3,	do.	do.		
		1849.				
71	James Fletcher...........	June 29,	Let. fr. ch. in Acton,			
72	Mrs. Eliza Duncan.........	Nov. 4,	Profession . . .			
		1850.				
73	Mrs. Elizabeth P. Putnam...	Jan. 6,	Letter from First Church.			
74	Mrs. Elizabeth A. Grosvenor.	6,	do.	do.		
75	Mrs. Sarah W. Putnam......	6,	do.	do.	Nov. 29, '55,	Dis. to Presb. ch., Gale-na, Ill.
76	Lydia M. Fletcher..........	6,	Let. fr. ch. Concord, N. H.			
77	Mrs. Henrietta M. Sears.....	May 26,	Let. fr. ch. in Wenham.		Jan. 29, '53,	Death.

78	Seth Butler	June 16,	Let. fr. ch. in Topsfield.	Dec. 11, '64,	Death.
79	Mrs. Mary Butler	16,	do. do.	Sept. 11, '52,	Death.
80	Mrs. Anna Drake	Oct. 4,	Let. fr. ch. in Wenham.	-, '58,	Death.
81	Mrs. Nancy Fish	Nov. 1, **1851.**	Let. fr. ch. in Middleton.	April 3, '63,	Dis. to ch. in No. Andover.
82	Edwin Perry	Feb. 28,	Letter from First Church.		
83	Mrs. Susan Cass	May 4,	Profession	Dec. 24, '54	Death.
84	Lydia A. Tapley	4,	do.		
85	Clara P. Fowler	Aug. 17,	do.		
86	Eliza K. Putnam	17,	do.	April 9, '61,	Death.
87	Emily Doherty,	17, **1852.**	do.	April 18, '64,	Dis. to ch. in So. Danvers.
88	Mrs. Jane Fulton	Mar. 7,	Letter from New York.		
89	Charles N. Ingalls	Nov. 5,	Let. fr. ch. in Holyoke.		
90	Mrs. Hannah A. Ingalls	Nov. 5, **1853.**	Let. from ch. in Holyoke.	Dec. 29, '68,	Death.
91	Mrs. Sally Demsey	**1854.**	Letter from First Church.		
92	Irving Stone	May 7,	Let. fr. M. E. ch. So. Danvers.		Dis. to South ch., Salem.
93	Nathaniel Hills	July 2,	Let. fr. ch. Gt. Falls, N.H.	65,	Dis. to ch. in Lynn.
94	Mrs. Mary A. Hills	2,	do. do.	65,	do. do.
95	Mrs. Louisa K. Putnam	Sept. 3,	Profession.	May 5, '61.	Dis. united with Epis.ch.

Chronological Record of Members—Continued.

Reg.	Names.	Date of Recep'n.	How Received.	Date of Removal.	How Removed.
96	Frederic C. Patterson	1854 Sept. 3,	Profession.	Mar. 21, '69.	Death.
97	Horace Drew	3,	do	Oct. 5, '55.	Dis. to ch. in Barring- ton. N. H.
98	Charles H. Learoyd	Nov. 5,	do.	Aug. 31, '60,	Dis. and united with Episcopal ch.
99	Addison P. Learoyd	5,	do.		
100	Samuel Page Fowler, Jr	5,	do.		
101	Matilda W. Porter	5,	do.	Oct. 9, '59,	Dis. to ch. in Plaistow, N. H.
102	Mary A. Pedrick	5,	do.		
103	Mrs. Sarah F. Brown	1855. Feb.	Let. fr. 4th ch, in Beverly.		
104	Anna R. Wilkins	May 6,	Profession.	Apr. 21, '61.	Dis. to Springfield St. ch.. Boston.
105	Mrs. Susannah Inman	1856. Jan. 13,	Let. fr. Ind. ch., Bradford, England.		
106	John S. Learoyd	1857. Feb. 1,	Profession.		
107	Mrs. Lydia F. Kimball	1,	do.		
108	Sarah S. Learoyd	1.	do.		
109	Emily G. Berry	1,	do.		
110	Caroline A. Perley	1,	do.		

No.	Name	Date		Admitted	Date Removed	How Removed
111	Maria A. Perley............	Feb.	1,	Profession.		
112	Louisa Tapley..............		1,	do.		
113	Martha Tapley..............		1,	do.		
114	Helen A. Putnam...........		1,	do.		
115	Hattie P. Fowler...........		1,	do.		
116	Mary Southwick............	July	5,	do.	Sept. 28, '64,	Death.
117	Mrs. Rhoda P. Brown.......		5,	do.		
118	Marshall C. Adams.........	Nov.	1,	Let. fr. ch., Burlington, Vt.	'64,	Dis. to ch. in Jaffrey, N. H.
119	Mrs. Susannah B. Adams...		1,	do.		do. do.
120	Daniel F. Savage..........		1,	Let. fr. ch., Amherst Col.	Dec. 5, '62,	Dis. to ch. in Cass, Io'a.
121	Samuel Wilson, Jr..........	1858. May	2,	Profession.		
122	Mrs. Helen A. Patterson....		2,	do.		
123	Mrs. Aphia H. Milliken.....		2,	do.		
124	Mrs. Sarah J. Straw........		2,	do.		
125	Mrs. Laura H. Perry........		2,	do.		
126	Abby W. Cass..............		2,	do.	April 2, '69,	Dis. to ch. Georgetown.
127	Harriet A. Elliott..........		2,	do.		
128	Augusta J. Brown..........		2,	do.		
129	Francis B. Patterson........		2,	do.	Oct. 23, '63,	Dis. to ch. in Natick.

Chronological Record of Members—Continued.

Reg.	Names.	Date of Recep'n.	How Received	Date of Removal.	How Removed.
		1858.			
130	Elias Savage...............	May 2,	Let. from ch. in Ipswich,	June 27, '65,	Death.
131	William Bradstreet, Jr......	2,	Let. from ch. in Topsfield,		
132	Mrs. Judith H. Bradstreet...	2,	do. do.		
133	Mrs. Hannah C. Perry......	2,	Let. fr. ch. in Middleton,		
134	Lorenzo D. Milliken.........	July 4,	Profession,		
135	Greenleaf P. Perley.........	4,	do.		
136	Louisa L. Putnam...........	4,	do.	Aug. 17, '61,	Death.
137	Mrs. Ellen E. Spofford	Nov. 7,	do,		
138	Augustine M. Spofford......	7,	Let. fr. ch. in Georgetown,		
139	J. H. Root.................	**1859.** July 3,	Let. fr. ch. in Byfield,	Feb. 9, '62,	Dis. to church in West Amesbury.
140	Rufus Putnam..............	Sept. 4,	Let. fr. Crombie st. ch., Salem.		
141	Mrs. Abigail Putnam........	4,	do. do.		
142	Elizabeth Putnam...........	4,	do. do.		
143	Mrs. Caroline Gould........	**1861.** May 5,	Letter from First Church,		
144	Alexander Leitch...........	**1862.**	Let. fr. ch. in Merrimack,		

No.	Name	Date	Mode of Admission	Date of Removal	Mode of Removal
145	Fullerton Leitch..............	1862.	Let. fr. ch. in Merrimack, N. H. do. do.		
146	Cathrine Leitch....	do. 1863.	do. do.	Sept. 30, '66,	Death.
147	Mary E. Hills..............	Mar. 1,	Profession.	Oct. 23, '63,	Death.
148	Mrs. Martha S. Putnam.....	Jan. 1,	Let. fr. ch. in Wenham,		
149	Sarah M. Richmond.........	Mar. 1,	Profession,	1864.	Dis. to First Church.
150	Annie J. Bradstreet........	1,	do.		
151	Henrietta Learoyd..........	1,	do.		
152	Abbie Glidden..............	1,	do.		
153	Laura M. Putnam........ ..	1,	do.		
154	Israel P. Black.............	1,	do.	1867.	Dis. to Pres. ch. in Belle Plains, Minn.
155	M. Alice Currier..........	May 3,	do.		
156	Lydia C. Currier............	3,	do.		
157	Mary E. Spaulding.........	3,	Let. fr. ch. in Dracut,		
158	Mrs. Martha A. Putnam.....	Nov. 1, 1864	Profession,		
159	William H. Edwards........	May 1,	do.		
160	Mrs. Dorcas P. Edwards.....	1, 1865.	do.		
161	Mrs. Anna G. Perley........	March.	do.		
162	John C. Proctor.............	Oct. 20, 1866.	Let. fr. ch. in Dart. Col.	July 1, 1870,	Dis. to ch. in Dart. Col.
163	Elbridge Trask....	July 1,	Profession,		

Chronological Record of Members—Continued.

Reg.	NAMES.	Date of Recep'n.	How Received.	Date of Removal.	How Removed.
		1866.			
164	Thomas M. Putnam.........	July 1,	Profession,		
165	Samuel P. Trask............	1,	do.		
166	George Carlton.............	1,	do.		
167	Horace M. Batson..........	1,	do.		
168	Mrs. Mary C. Legroo........	1,	do.		
169	Carrie E. Welch......... .	1,	do.		
170	Martha I. Mason...........	1,	do.		
171	Hattie A. P. Putnam........	1,	do.		
172	Sarah A. Bradstreet........	1,	do.	June 1, '68,	Dis. to Presbt. ch. in Portchester, N. Y.
173	Helen A. Elliot.............	1,	do.		
174	Mrs. Mary J. Glidden.......	1,	do.		
175	Mrs. Louisa P. Weston......	1,	do.		
176	Mrs. Martha M. Allen.......	1,	do.		
177	Mrs. Eliza C. Pope..........	1,	do.		

179	Mrs. Sophia E. Inman	July	1,	Profession.		
180	Mary C. Currier		1,	do.		
181	Nancy C. Dodge		1,	do.		
182	Mrs. Sarah L. Trask		1,	do.		
183	Mrs. Sarah A. Baker		1,	do.		
184	William A. Bradstreet		1,	do.		
185	John B. Frost		1,	do.		
186	Herbert M. Bradstreet		1,	do.		
187	James C. Dougherty		1,	do.		
188	James O. Perry		1,	do.		
189	Wallace P. Perry		1,	do.		
190	George E. Fuller		1,	do.		
191	Charles P. Fuller		1,	do.		
192	James M. Dudley		1,	do.		
193	Louis N. Wilkins		1,	do.	1867.	Dis. united with Bap.ch.
194	Helen M. Dudley		1,	do.	1870.	Dis. united with M.E.ch. Salem.
195	Sarah E. Baker		1,	do.		
196	M. Ella Sheldon		1,	do.		

Chronological Record of Members—Continued.

Reg.	NAMES.	Date of Recep'n.	How Received.	Date of Removal.	How Removed.
		1866.			
197	Mercy A. Perry..............	July 1,	Profession.		
198	Ellen E. Wilkins............	1,	do.		
199	Harriet E. Sheldon..........	1,	do.		
200	Emma J. Bradstreet........	1,	do.		
201	Annie Learoyd..............	1,	do.		
202	Myra P. Trask..............	1,	do.		
203	Carrie W. Trask............	1,	do.		
204	S. Agnes Putnam...........	1,	do.		
205	Jane E. Crowther..........	1,	do.		
206	Mary W. Fletcher..........	1,	do.		
207	A. Susan Patterson........	1,	do.		
208	Albion S. Dudley..........	1,	do.		
209	Thomas E. Dougherty.......	1,	do.		

No.	Name	Date		Received	Date	Remarks
211	Mrs. Ruth A. Cook	July	1,	Profession.		
212	Caroline Learoyd		1,	do.		
213	Harriet E. Elliot		1,	do.		
214	Mrs. Harriet S. Emerson		1,	Letter from First Church.		
215	James Martin		1,	Let. fr. ch. in Manchester, N. H.		
216	Mrs. J. Martin		1,	do. do.		
217	Elijah Bradstreet		1,	Let. fr. ch. in Topsfield,		
218	Mrs. Ellen M. Bradstreet		1,	do. do.		
219	Eben Peabody		1,	do. do.		
220	Mrs. Ellen M. Eaton		1,	do. do.		
221	Thomas F. Ferguson		1,	do. do.		
222	Mrs. Sarah A. Ferguson		1,	do. do.		
223	Robert S. Perkins		1,	do. do.		
224	Mrs. Nancy Bradstreet		1,	do. do.		
225	William Carruthers	July	1,	Let. fr. ch. No. Cambr'ge.	Apr. 2, '69,	Dis. to ch. in Calais, Me.
226	Mrs. Mary L. Carruthers		1,	do. do.	Apr. 2, '69,	Dis. to ch. in Calais, Me.
227	Mary E. Porter	Sept.	3,	Profession,		
228	Clara E. Putnam		3,	do.		

Chronological Record of Members—Continued.

Reg.	NAMES.	Date of Recep'n.	How Received.	Date of Removal.	How Removed.
229	Nathaniel Batson...........	3,	Let. fr. ch. in Newcastle, N. H.		
230	Maria T. Knight.....	3,	Profession,		
231	Ruth A. Phelps.	3,	do.		
232	Mary C. Putnam............	3,	do.		
233	Mrs. Abigail L. Elliot.......	3,	do.		
234	Mrs. Margaret P. Butler.....	3,	do.		
235	Mrs. Mary A. Langley.......	3,	do.		
236	Mrs. Nancy P. Fellows......	3,	do.		
237	Mrs. Mary W. Putnam......	3,	do.		
238	Mrs. Ellen Henderson.......	3,	do.		
239	Mrs. Mary Tufts............	3,	do.		
240	Mrs. Mary Dodge...........	3,	do.		
241	Edward A. Lord....	3,	do.		

243	Mrs. Martha J. Sawyer	Sept.	3,	Profession,		
244	Azubah A. Kimball		3,	do.		
245	Charlotte Turner		3,	do.		
246	Mary E. Tufts		3,	do.		
247	Mary J. Goodwin		3,	do.		
248	C. Emma Sawyer		3,	do.		
249	Marrietta E. Sawyer		3,	do.		
250	Josephine A. Andrews		3,	do.		
251	Lucinda Pray		3,	do.		
252	William P. Perkins		3,	do.		
253	George W. Ingalls		3,	do.		
254	Francis Ingalls		3,	do.		
255	William H. Edwards		3,	do.		
256	Jonas Fiske		3,	Let. fr. ch. in Salem,		
257	Mrs. Abigail Fiske		3,	do. do.		
258	Mrs. Lucy Clough	Nov.	4,	Profession,	April 23, 1868.	Dis. joined M. E. ch. E. Boston.
259	Henry Perry		4,	do.		
260	M. Angie Legroo		4,	do.		

Chronological Record of Members—Continued.

Reg.	Names.	Date of Recep'n.	How Received.	Date of Removal.	How Removed.
261	Mrs. E. H. Lane............	1866. Nov. 4,	Letter.		
262	Mrs. Mary E. Peabody	1867. May 5.	Letter from ch. in Essex,		
263	Nathan T. Putnam..	July	Profession.		
264	Emily Allen	July	do.		
265	Caroline O. Brown.........	July	do.		
266	Edwin Tufts...............	1868. March 1,	do.	May 1, '68,	Dis. joined M. E. ch. Peabody.
267	Flora A. Putnam...........	1,	do.		
268	Mrs. D. H. Caldwell........	1.	do.	Aug. 17, '68,	Dis. to Dane st. ch. Bev.
269	J. Adams Welch......	June, '67	do.		
270	Mrs. Sarah A. Bomer........	Jan. 21,	Let. fr. ch. Wheelock, N. H.		
271	G. W. Fiske...............	Dec. '68,	Letter fr. ch. in Groton,		
272	Mrs. Sarah Fiske...........	Dec. '68,	do. do.		
273	Mrs. Asenath P. Tapley.....	1869. May 1,	Letter from First Church,		
274	Henry L. Eaton............	Oct. 15,	Let. fr. ch. in Wakefield,		

No.	Name	Date	Admitted	Removed
276	Mrs. Hannah F. Perry	Oct. 15,	Let. fr. Bap. ch. Danvers Port.	
277	James Brand	15,	Let. fr. ch. Yale College,	
278	Mrs. Mary E. Guilford	Nov. 7,	Profession.	
279	Ora F. Staples	7,	do.	
280	Mrs. Margaret Brennan	7,	do.	
281	George W. Andrews	1870. March 6,	do.	
282	Mrs. Amelia Lawson	6,	do.	
283	Mrs. Elizabeth Peabody	6,	Let. fr. Crombie st. ch., Salem.	
284	Carrie W. Wilson	May 1,	Let. fr. ch. Sullivan, N.H.	
285	Mrs. Carrie E. Pray	1,	Let. fr. M.E. ch. Topsfield,	
286	Mary E. Dougherty	July 3,	Profession.	
287	Mrs. Mary Cuthbertson	3,	do.	
288	Mrs. Joanna Emerson	3,	do.	
289	Anna F. Hicks	3,	do.	
290	Samuel W. Durgin	3,	do.	
291	Horace S. Rundlett	3,	do.	
292	Mrs. Minerva B. Sanborn	3,	do.	
293	Perley M. Whipple	3,	do.	Dec. 7, '70, Death.
294	Alice E. Learoyd	3,	do.	

Chronological List of Members—Continued.

Reg.	Names.	Date of Recep'n.	How Received.	Date of Removal.	How Removed.
		1870.			
295	Addie L. Fowle.............	July 3,	Profession.		
296	Mary E. Cummings.........	3,	do.		
297	Mrs. Maria E. Bradstreet....	3,	do.		
298	Mrs. Sarah J. Wright.......	3,	do.		
299	Mrs. Harriet A. White......	3,	do.		
300	Frederick Wright	3,	do.		
301	Abram S. Beal.............	3,	do.		
302	Nathan B. Patterson........	3,	do.		
303	John E. Dow..............	3,	do.		
304	Mrs. Lydia W. Gould.......	3,	do.		
305	Ella M. Elliott	3,	do.		
306	Charles L. Elliott.	3,	do.		
307	James M. Sawyer..........	3,	do.		
308	E. Warren Eaton..........	3,	do.		

No.	Name	Date		Mode of Admission	Remarks
310	Mrs. Sarah J. Ripley	July	3,	Profession,	
311	Mrs. Lucinda E. Hall,		3,	do.	
312	Sarah E. Putnam		3,	do.	
313	Abbie M. Perkins		3,	do.	
314	George S. Perry		3,	do.	
315	Mrs. Mary E. McIntire		3,	do.	
316	Nellie L. Bean		3,	do.	
317	Alice S. Pettengill		3,	do.	
318	Emily Pope		3,	do.	June 9, '71, Dis. to ch. in Peabody.
319	Harriet H. Glidden		3,	do.	
320	Mrs. Sarah E. Ridley		3,	Let. fr. M. E. ch. in Lynn,	
321	Mrs. Jane Leitch		3,	Let. fr. Elliot ch. Roxbury,	
322	Mrs. Julia M. Perkins		3,	Let fr. ch. in Boxford,	
323	Mrs. Sarah Perry		3,	Let. fr, First ch. Danvers,	
324	Horatio Perry		3,	do. do.	
325	Ellen T. Du Bois	Nov.	6,	Profession,	
326	Mrs. Esther A. Patterson		6,	do.	
327	Mrs. Lucy A. Durgin		6,	do.	
328	Mrs. Sarah E. Hooper		6,	do.	

Chronological Record of Members—Continued.

Reg.	Names.	Date of Recep'n.	How Received.	Date of Removal.	How Removed.
		1870.			
329	Hannah E. Pedrick..........	Nov. 6,	Profession,		
330	Lyman Ridley..............	6,	do.		
331	Nellie Hill.....	6,	do.		
332	Edward H. Holley..........	6,	do.		
		1871.			
333	Daniel Gould..............	Jan. 1,	do.		
334	Samuel Miller.............	1,	do.		
335	Jeremiah Crowther.........	1,	do.		
336	Samuel L. Sawyer..........	1,	Let. fr. ch. in Boxford,		
337	Mrs. Nellie B. Sawyer......	1,	do. do.		
338	Lucretia J. Allen...........	1,	Let. from Phillips ch., So. Boston.		
339	Mrs. Sarah C. Putnam	1,	Let. fr. First ch. Danvers,		
340	Mrs. Elizabeth O. Whiting..	1,	Let. fr. ch. in Charlton,		
341	Mrs. Laura A. Miller........	March 5,	Profession,		
342	Mrs. Elizabeth C. Edwards..	5,	Let. fr. Crombie st. ch. in Salem.		
343	J. Franklin Bly......	5,	Let. fr. ch. No. Haverhill		

344	Mrs. Matilda W. Bly	March 5,	Let. fr. ch. No. Haverhill,		
345	Mrs. Asenath A. Berry	May 7,	Profession,		
346	Isaac A. Berry	7,	do.		
347	Hattie J. Perkins	7,	do.		
348	Flora J. Robinson	7,	do.		
349	Theophilus C. Everett	7,	do.		
350	Mrs. Mary A. Everett	7,	do.		
351	Richard Tolman	May '45,	Let. fr. ch. in Dorchester,	April 22, '49,	Dis. to ch. So. Dennis.
352	Mrs. Charlotte Williams	July 2,	Let. fr. ch. Pubnico, N. S.		
353	Mrs. Phebe R. Danforth	2,	Let. fr. ch. in Peabody.		
354	Mrs. Lydia Pettengill	2,	Letter from First Church.		
355	Ella Maria Bradstreet	2,	Profession.		

QUESTIONS.

1. Are you in the practice of daily secret prayer?

2. Are you in the practice of daily family prayer?

3. Do you daily, with a prayerful desire to improve in christian knowledge, read the word of God?

4. Do you make it a matter of conscience to attend all the meetings for social worship appointed by the church, when the providence of God allows?

5. Do you pray every day, that God will bless his truth to the conversion of sinners?

6. Do you do conscientiously what you can, by your pecuniary ability, to promote the kingdom of Christ?

7. Are you as tender of the reputation of a brother as of your own?

8. Do you cultivate a spirit of tenderness and christian charity toward the failings and imperfections of your brethren?

9. Do you feel it to be your solemn duty to consecrate all you have and are to the Lord?

10. Will you daily ask God to help you keep the covenant you have made with him and the church?